POVERTY KILLS TOO!

JESSICA DEANNA

Introduction

As a Christian, it is exciting to write a book that highlights the Church Experience. Having a real voice that's unapologetically authentic, Kind Jackson is the main character in this story who experiences multiple heart breaks from her parents, chruch family and death of her loved ones. You will read about how growing up in poverty is a pipeline to prison.

CHAPTER 1:

Sundays Best

Does *poverty* kill? I used to love getting up on Sunday mornings.

Just because it was church. The church was one of my favorite places to go. Most of the children at church had empathy. The church was a safe place for my self-esteem. Living in the projects was not a safe place for anyone! Most children lacked empathy and would tease you if you did not wear the latest fashion. Pastor Turner was a father to fatherless children. Church dinners were the best when Mama could afford them. Most of all, old people were nice to children, plenty of hugs, peppermint, and butterscotch. Lastly, I sang lead for most of the songs for the children's choir. I love how my voice gave people that special feeling about the Lord. This service was like no other. This church service was booming with happy feet. Like one big family, we clapped our hands to the rhythm of the beat. You could feel the floor vibrating from the bass of the music. The rhythm coursed through our clothes, the atmosphere; it filled everyone with the Holy Spirit.

As I sang, leading the choir, I was reminded of how I could not wait to meet King Jesus. Although, some people thought my singing was well... interesting, I could care less. All that matters is that I would sing for the lord out of the purity of my heart. Then one day, I started to question my faith.

CHAPTER 2:

The Affair

Saturday had arrived—the day designated for choir rehearsals. I was in the bathroom stall and overheard a conversation between Tammy, a church member who served on the nurse board, and her mother Brenda, who also served on the nurses' board. Whenever I see Brenda in her nurse uniform, I swear it looks like it is going to tear. Especially when she would bend down to grab something. Brenda is far from petite, but she is not fat either. Brenda made the best homemade mac and cheese and ran the church with gifted cooking. But the mother and daughter were talking about my mother. My own mother!

"I hate Valerie," Tammy said with an angry tone.

"Tammy, it'll be fine. I will talk to Pastor Turner about it. You know Pastor Turner does not tolerate this kind of mess within the church. He will take care of it," Brenda said reassuring her, trying to convince her and calm her down.

"I can't believe Darnell would do this to me, have an affair, Mama. Valire? Freaking Valire disgusting ass from the projects. I swear them people up there do anything just to have a man. That's exactly why they are single mothers with multiple baby daddies," said Tammy ranting.

I could feel my blood boiling as I sat in the stall listening. *I mean how could...how could that...that ugh talk all that about my mama*, I thought to myself.

It took every ounce of patience within me to not jump out of my stall and curse their asses out without delay. I am quite sure Pastor Turner is going to side with Miss Brenda and her daughter. They always got their way when it came to the pastor. Tammy kept venting to her mom.

"Mama, the church should ban them. Shameless women who have no respect for themselves coming up in here with their bodies on display and all the kids they bring," Tammy complained, earning a hush in response. "Them Jezebels should be locked up. They come to steal and destroy families by sleeping with husbands and fathers," Tammy said with frustration.

"Don't worry. Mama is going to fix it as soon as the pastor gets back."

"You sure Pastor Turner is goanna be here on Saturday, Mama?" Tammy question.

"Yes, baby, you know he doesn't allow anyone else to lock the church up. Don't worry, baby."

I just sat there looking at my beautiful mother's face, trying to get past the fact that she herself broke one of the Ten Commandments, "Thou shalt not commit adultery." I deviated my thoughts and focused back on Tammy. I thought about her and Mr. Darnell and how they were unable to have kids. Every day I prayed for them. Miss Tammy was not an attractive woman, but she was a genuinely nice lady who dressed respectably—unlike my mama who always wore tight clothes to show her nicely shaped figure. Sometimes, she would not even wear underwear even though she wore a see-through dress. This never made Daddy happy. She would often earn the attention of the ushers who would pull her to the side about her inappropriate attire. What kills me is that Miss Tammy does not know about Daddy and the fact that all three of her kids are his. I must admit, my mama is not nice to my daddy. I should tell him Mama is having an affair, then, Miss Brenda would not have to tell Pastor Turner. Daddy would be able to settle things down.

CHAPTER 3:

Living In The Projects

The next morning, my mama as usual called for me to make breakfast for everyone. Being the oldest of the three kids, I was automatically given the role of being a mother to my younger siblings. Like the little mother I am, I would have to get them dressed and prepare breakfast for them. I would spend so much time on them that I always found myself scurrying to get ready myself. It would have been nice if Mama helped a little. But my mama had her own self to take care of. She focused on keeping her Halle Berry cut freshly done every week by one of the best Chicago stylists. Whenever I would go with Mama, Trina the stylist, would always ask Mama when she would let her do something with my beautiful thick hair. Mama always had a lie prepared. Trina knew Mama was lying but would just let it slide. She knew and I knew that my mama takes the welfare checks and spend it on herself or Daddy. All we used to get is mothball-smelling clothes from Goodwill on discount days. I always pictured myself as being a Black Cinderella in every way. Mama already had me take care of my siblings, and I always did all the cleaning in the house. I hand wash my brother and sister clothes in the tub whenever we have soap. Mama keeps most of the toiletries locked up in her room out of fear that I might waste them when cleaning.

Most of the kids that live in the projects with us aren't getting their basic needs met either. We all have dirty clothes to match and uncombed hair. The only kids who stayed fly were the ones whose mama's boyfriends sold dope. I would count the days I would be able to escape from this hellhole. If I must sell dope in order to leave, I will. But I would never stoop so low to sell my body. All our mamas get food stamps, and almost all of us have step daddies who are unemployed and who use our mamas to have free food and a roof over their heads. Although they are unemployed, they are professional naggers and verbal abusers to the women and kids, which ultimately ruined our self-esteem. They would shame us for living in the projects although they were living in it with us. The only man I've seen take care of his family comes on TV on Thursday nights—Bill Cosby. I'd watch Bill Cosby's kids in awe of how beautiful they always looked in their clean puffy dresses and styled hair. I was dirt compared to them because I didn't have the clothes, I needed to look as fashionable. My clothes were always two sizes big on me. But I guess the only beauty I found in myself was my caramel clear skin. I believe I got my looks from my daddy. We have the same complexion. I don't have acne like the rest of my friends my age, and Mama never let us drink pop. We always drank plenty of water mainly because it was free. I admired my full plump lips, perfectly shaped nose, brown eyes, and height. I'm five feet tall which is tall for a fifteen-year-old. If you ask me, I got my height from my six feet three inches tall Daddy. I have a slender shape which didn't draw any attention compared to the girls in the building who had nice booties and were lighter skinned.

My little sister, Star, who is nine years old, has hair straight from the motherland. Everyone calls her light bright because she's light-skinned, just like my mama, with nappy hair. Being light-colored seemed right in the projects. You always got things handed to you.

My brother, Leo, is six years old and is also light like my mama, but he doesn't look like us. Granny would say he looks like her brother who died in a fire when they were younger. I was really dreading going back to church after what I heard the other day, but I had a solo recital that was going to lead. Luckily, I didn't see Miss Tammy, her husband, Darnell, or Brenda. I was wondering what might have happened with Pastor Turner yesterday. My mom seemed happy and looked beautiful, but she would've been even prettier if she didn't dress like a tramp. Mama and Daddy would get along more if Mama started dressing more appropriately. The men in the neighborhood always noticed her, and one time, a man called her Coca-Cola, because of her figure, I guess. I zoned back into my surroundings and realized I was standing on stage in front of the church members. I had everyone standing to their feet and began singing about heaven, hoping that Mama would pay some attention, but I highly doubted it. Every so often, I looked at Pastor Turner's family in the audience looking perfect. They were always the best dressed and were one of the few people in the church who had cars. Many of us came to church on a bus or walked. I began to feel my stomach growl and couldn't help but lose focus on what I was singing. I started reminiscing about the delicious food waiting for me that the church often sold after every service. We could never afford the food but couldn't help but wonder why the church sells the food instead of giving it to us for free. We always pay our tithes after Pastor Turner's usual lengthy speeches saying, "Give and you will be blessed even more," even though most of the church members are jobless. I mean I thought the church is supposed to feed the less fortunate. It wouldn't hurt to give us a free meal every now and then. Well, sometimes Mr. Darnell would give me money to buy food after I sang a solo, but Mama would usually take the money from me so he would often reward me by buying the food himself for me instead. He is a nice guy.

My mind wandered about adults. Was God made up as a way for parents to have their kids behave? If so, then why? I see a lot of adults take part in all kinds of sinful things in God's house, like smoking cigarettes near the building after church. I normally see Deacon Brogan on my way to rehearsal, before the afternoon service, going to the liquor store. He hides it in his steel water bottle and takes sips from it during Pastor Turner's sermons. Sometimes, I question God's existence. Like, when is he going to talk to me like he does with Pastor Turner? Does God only talk to pastors?

Daddy was upset when my Mama, my brother, and my sister arrived home from church. He and Mama got into a heated argument. I heard it from my room.

"You can't even make sure your husband eats first. You are too busy worshipping a white Jesus and paying a pimp pastor. Your duty is to your home. You hear me? I don't know much about God, but this house comes first!" Daddy said to my mom with rage.

"Maybe if you came to church and wasn't always such an ass, we would have Sunday dinner," my Mama shot back at him.

He fired back fueling the fire, "I'm not going to church to get brainwashed by some pimp pastor."

If only Monday could come by quicker. Mama and Daddy's argument was like a daily lullaby that put me to sleep. I just wanted us to be like the normal one big happy family. No arguments. No complaining. No negativity. Just a family of five who enjoyed each other's company, but Mama and Daddy never acted like a married couple. Sometimes I think Daddy secretly hates Mama or is jealous that everywhere she goes, everyone wants her attention but not his. Come to think of it, I've never heard Daddy tell Mama she was beautiful or much less compliment her in any way. This was something I often heard a stranger doing instead of Daddy. I can understand why Mama likes it when a man like Darnell tells her how beautiful she is. Daddy only verbally expressed Mom's flaws to her. I felt my eyes growing heavy and quickly found myself drifting asleep slowly then, all at once.

CHAPTER 4:

Welfare Check

The next morning, I woke up to chaos. My siblings and I were running late for school. I quickly woke Star and Leo up and helped them get ready before they missed the school breakfast. To make matters worse, I found that Leo wet his bed, and I had to bathe him to find we had no soap. I just had to manage with what I had and get us ready. I didn't have time to beg Mama for the soap, as she kept it locked away in her room. Ugh, I can't wait for us to get our food stamps, so we don't have to rush to school to have breakfast and eat at home, and I always wonder why we must go to the currency exchange to pick the food stamps up. One time, I went to the currency exchange with Mama, and it smelled and looked like a zoo. It was as if nobody had taken a bath in months. It was pure straight up B.O. Everyone dragged themselves around in their pajamas.

I always feel like I'm the parent. Isn't it the adult's job to care of their kids? Yes, I understand I'm the oldest sibling, but she's supposed to be the mother, not me. Daddy could at least help; he's always at home. I've never even seen him go to work. I could always count on daddy to leave out the house on the third of the month. That was Mama's welfare check day. He is always happy on that day. He goes to the store and pick his favorite cereal that we can't touch. Mama gives him half of the welfare check she gets from the currency exchange. She believes Daddy should get half of the money since we're his kids, but one time, Mama went shopping with her best friend, Sheila. My father paced the floor all day. When Mama got back, and she spent the welfare check, it was Mike Tyson lights out for Mama. Mama face was swollen from daddy beating. Leo cried all night. She makes sure now Daddy get his half. He spends it all at Rothschilds where he gets drinks with his best friend, Tim. Tim and Daddy have been friends since childhood. Tim is like an uncle to us, but often, I catch him checking out Mama. I assume the welfare check was to help needy mothers who didn't have help from the deadbeat dads, but the deadbeats still live with the mothers. Fathers who never sign birth certificates. Out of fear paying child support. When inspection comes, the fathers have to hide their shoes and clothes. What type of dignity is that. Most of us never have our daddy last name.Breed them and can't feed them is all you get growing up in the buildings. I am never lowering my standards just to have a man. Really, what are boyfriends and husbands for when they just lay around nagging and doing nothing with their lives? Crazy, all they do is make babies, so the welfare check can keep rolling in.

CHAPTER 5:

My Girls

All I want to do is hangout with my two best friends, Nicole and Diamond. Nicole is very pretty. She is mixed with Arab and Black. Her mama is with one of the Arab men at Mike's corner store. That's where her mama gets most of her money. Nicole always gets new Jordan's every two months. I on the other hand wear Xj100s, which are the imitation Jordan's gym shoes. My mama does most of our shopping at the thrift store where she usually embarrasses me on 50 percent off days hauling out large bags from the thrift store.

It's as if she bought everything the store sold. But Diamond and Nicole always made me feel better and looked out for me. Nicole usually tries to give me her hand-me-downs, but I would never take them because they would be better served in charity. Diamond also always stayed fly even though she was nowhere near looked like a diamond. Maybe that's the reason her mom dresses her so nice. You know, to balance things, I guess. Her being light-skinned is the only thing she has going for her. She's even bald headed. But her big booty compensates for her bald head. That always has grown men looking. A big booty is a golden ticket in the hood. It especially grabbed the attention of Red, who is one of the dealers. Diamond also had big front buck teeth that would get in the way of her closing her mouth. My Mama said her mom should buy her braces instead of all the expensive clothes she wears. But my friends are my friends, and I wouldn't trade them for the world. We always have each other's back, and no one dares messes with us.

In church, we are taught to fear God and be nice, but the kids in my neighborhood do not know anything about God. All they know is gang signs, guns, and drugs. Red told me, Diamond, and Nicole that we could hold drugs for him. That is how the drug dealers get away with what they do. They use children like us to stash their drugs. Some of the children are used to selling the drugs for them. Most of the children they used were boys. It was rare for them to use females, even though police hardly check the young girls. Anyways, Red said we could be making one hundred fifty dollars a week, and I was down for that. So, my friends and I came up with our gang's name, SAB, aka Sticking All Bitches. When we met up with Red, he gave us the rundown of how things will work. I stashed the drugs in a zip lock bag in my underwear. Nicole held the drugs in her mouth. Diamond did not have to do anything, since Red and her had a relationship thing going on, even though she was fifteen and he is twenty-seven. The first week was a success. We each made one hundred fifty dollars, which I spent all on my personal needs, so I could take care of myself. One day, I was out doing business as usual when I bumped into our neighbor Elijah. He was talking about how my daddy is going to kill me if he ever found out. Geez, that man can be so nosy. I used to hang with his nephew Jay till he was killed in a drive by. Occasionally, Elijah would send me on errands to the store for his mom and would allow me to keep the change that is why I let his comment slide. I swear sometimes it felt like he was flirting with me.

"Kind, I didn't know you was the type to be slanging in the streets. You should have come to me first. You know I got my own corner too. I could have put you on. I mean, let me know if you need anything," Elijah continued at me.

My squad and I were making money. We feel so popular whenever Red would pick us up from school in his luxury SUV. He would drop me off at Trina's shop where I continued my side hustle of cleaning the beauty shop as a cover-up for my parents. My pay was fifty a week, which is really not bad, just more money for me. After I finished, I asked Trina if she could straighten my hair, and she agreed. I finally got my hair done for once. Damn, having your own money sure is good. When she turned me around toward the mirror, I was speechless.

"You look gorgeous. Now I can see why your mama did not let you get your hair done. All of them boys would've been hollering at you, girl."

Elijah came into the shop and glanced over to me and Trina.

"You know Kind, Elijah?"

"This is the little girl I was telling you about who comes and keeps the shop clean for me. Kind and your son Jay used to always walk with each other to school," Elijah explained with excitement to Trina.

I felt so bad for Trina. No mother should ever have to lose their son. Trina's a strong lady.

"I'm so sorry, Miss Trina," I said expressing my condolences.

"It's okay, baby," she said with a bit of shakiness in her voice.

"It's a small world, Kind. You're well cared for with my big sister," Elijah said.

"Elijah can you make sure Kind get home safely? You know these thirsty niggas out here," Trina asked with disgust.

"Are you okay with taking a ride to 63rd Hasted," he politely asked me.

"Yeah," I responded, unsure of myself.

"Don't worry, we won't be long. I just want to get an outfit for Henry's party tonight," he explained.

I was also trying to go to the party. The leather in Elijah's black Monte Carlo smelled so good. He had great music taste as well. He was playing "Cry for you." by Jodeci. I found a beautiful Tommy Hilfiger outfit at the store. But to my surprise, Elijah bought it for me even though I was just admiring it.

I offered to pay for myself because I had my own money, but Elijah refused and said something like, "A true man would never let a lady pay." I felt like he was flirting with me again. I took in my surroundings and noticed that Trina was right. There were grown men giving me the looks. Elijah noticed the attention I was getting as well.

"These niggas are all over you girl. And you know the niggas in the building love some young girls, especially with that new hair look my sister gave you. You better watch out for them. Don't let their sweet talk fool you though," Elijah explained with worry.

CHAPTER 6:

Daddy Left Home

When I arrived home, I found my daddy doing his usual drinking with Tim and listening to music by The Isley Brothers. I was still trying to figure out a way how I would be able to go to Henry's party without Daddy finding out. Things were getting intense at home between Mama and Daddy. Daddy started giving Mama a curfew when she would go out with her friend Sheila.

I took a bath and dressed myself in preparation to sneak off to the party. As soon as I set foot out of the bathroom, my daddy was right there questioning me.

"Where the fuck do you think you're going? You got school tomorrow. You trying to be a tramp like your mama?"

"Tomorrow's the last day of school and nobody goes. Mama said I could go to the party," I explained.

"Well, not tonight, you slut. Mama isn't here. She probably somewhere fucking some Pastor," he said with a slurred speech.

He was obviously drunk and could barely hold himself up. I angrily stomped to my room and slammed the door behind me. I hate my dad so much. I thought about Leo and the fact that he would never say that to me.

But I would always forgive Dad no matter what he might have said or did to me. Ten minutes later, I could hear Mama and Sheila stumble inside the house drunk. I came out the room to check up on them and to kind of show them my new look. I did a little twirl and showed her my new hairdo, and she even complimented me.

"Oh, Kind, you look beautiful," Mama said in awe.

"Thank you, Mama. You really like it?" I asked.

"It's beautiful," Mama reassured me.

I handed Mama thirty dollars. "Here you go, Mama, for you. I want to give you a little something from my paycheck."

"Oh baby, you didn't have to do this… Thank you though," Mama said with her slurred drunken speech. She lazily threw her arms around me for a hug and nearly collapsed on me. I helped her take a seat on the couch. Sheila took a seat beside her as well.

"You're more useful than your sorry-ass daddy," Mama complained.

Mama took a deep breath, then raised her eyebrows as if having an epiphany.

"Why aren't you at the party, Kind?

"Daddy said I can't go because I have school the next day," I explained.

"Fuck your daddy. Go to the party. But do not go out there messing with them boys. I am not ready to be a Grandma," Mama said.

Sheila busted out in laughter after she heard that, and Mama joined in. I wanted to go to the party, but I didn't want to try and cause more trouble in the house and break my family up. I arrived at the party, and it was packed with practically everyone in the neighborhood and school. R. Kelly song was blasting in the atmosphere, "Hey Mr. DJ." All eyes were on me when I came in. Nicole and Diamond rushed over to me and bombarded me with hugs. Henry came over and called me, "Sis!!" He's Nicole's crazy boyfriend. He earns himself some money, but he's a known killer. We had fun and had a few light drinks or two. Things were beginning to wind down. We were about to head out when we bumped into Elijah.

"It's time to get you home, Kind. Your mama and daddy had a fight at the house," Elijah insisted.

"What happened? Is she ok?" I desperately asked.

I told Nicole and Diamond I have to leave early and made my way out of the party with Elijah. When I got home, I found Mama crying. She had a black eye, and her lip was busted too. Leo and Star were sitting on the couch beside her in tears. I rushed over and asked what happened.

"Daddy did this, and Uncle Tim didn't stop him," Leo said speaking for Mama.

"Uncle Tim isn't your Uncle, Leo," I spat back at him with anger. I realized what I did and quickly regretted it. I apologized. I was so overwhelmed with emotions I didn't know what to do with myself, so I ran off into the kitchen to find the whole place had been ransacked. There were broken dishes everywhere. I let out a silent cry and started cleaning up the mess. I stayed up all night, cleaning the house up while Mama, Leo, and Star rested on the couch. I could not believe my Daddy. I mentally cursed him out with every curse word I could think of.

Later the next morning, I went over to Mikes and got some groceries and stuff for the house. I made the house bacon, eggs, and potatoes, and everyone woke up to the aroma of the food. Mama came into the kitchen, and I saw that he had horribly bruised up her face. It got worse and wanted to make me cry, but I had to be strong for Mama. I made her a plate of breakfast and went to get Leo and Star ready for school. We went outside early, so I could make more money, and I stumbled upon Henry again. Henry is a true hustler, and if he doesn't get killed or go to jail, he could honestly be the next big drug dealer around here. I must admit, sometimes I'm scared to be seen with him, as he's very unpredictable. He's always had his gun on him. I never want to stick around to find out what he will do or get caught up in a crossfire.

"How is your mama doing, Kind? I heard she was..."

I interrupt him and quickly respond, "Yeah, she's doing fine. Thanks."

"Alright, let me know if you need anything. We family now since me and your girl Nicole official," Henry said jokingly.

"You could give me some more dope to sell," I politely asked.

"I got you, Kind. Give me about a week."

CHAPTER 7:

Mr. Darnell

Weeks had passed, and Daddy never came back home. Mama gathered us into the living room for one of her family meetings and told us that her Fiancé Darnell is moving in. Guess what? The next day, Darnell moved in. I had never seen Mama so happy before. I minded my own business and continued to keep the house clean. I took Leo and Star outside with me till seven in the evening and went back out at ten in the night alone to sell drugs Mama was so oblivious to what I was doing. I had accepted that she really doesn't care. She didn't care to know how I was able to afford the food that I brought home. But she did assume that I was sleeping with Elijah and threatened to put me on birth control. She even confronted Elijah about it. Mama think

I am a hoe, but little does she know I am an independent hustler working with Elijah. I do feel like Elijah had me working with him so he could keep a better eye on me. I can't keep lying to myself. Elijah is a fine tall chocolate man. All the ladies want him, and he has such a sexy deep voice. He's built like a professional football player. He is an attractive lady's man, but I never see him hanging out with many women. Working closer to Elijah gave me street credibility, since I don't know street sales as he does.

I was starting to lose respect for my daddy. Why couldn't he be kind and loving to Mamma and make his kids happy and play with us? I can tell you this, I love working more for Elijah than I did for Red because Elijah took care of me like he is my big brother. He even got me better glasses.

When Trina found out that I was selling crack, she tried to convince me to stop, "Drug money is fast and additive." So, she stopped doing my hair. I've found someone else to do my hair though—Tikka. She is kind but, at times, she can be cold to me. Elijah doesn't like it when I get my hair done, though, because he thinks I'm supposed to look broke. He tried flirting with me too, but I am not dumb enough to fall for his games. He said something like, "If you want to be Miss Pretty Girl, then you need to be my woman, and you don't have to stand on the block." I told him that I'd rather make my own money.

I went home and put my hair in a ponytail and put on some of my old clothes. I was starting to think Elijah was right. I was losing focus on this material shit. I did not need to bring no heat with 5.0 in the neighborhood. I needed to stay low-key if I didn't not want to draw any attention from the police.

Later I ran into my Daddy at Mike's cornerstone.

"You are coming back home, Daddy?" I asked.

"No, baby girl. Just picking up a few things," he responded with a bit of guilt in his voice.

"Oh...Daddy, where do you live?" I asked with hesitation.

"I'm staying with your granny till I get a job. Then I'll come get you guys. How's church?"

"I don't think Mama believes in church anymore," I hopelessly said.

"Well, make sure to continue going to your choir practices and take your brother and sister with you to the services," Daddy said.

I was surprised that Daddy even brought up church, since he never really went.

"God is real. You hear, my girl," he added.

"Yes, Daddy. Bad company ruins good moral. That's in the Bible," I reassured him.

"I know your Mama isn't doing her job but remember to do the right thing. Don't forget, God sees everything."

"Daddy, I didn't know you believed in church," I stated.

He explained, "Kind Jackson, you don't believe in church. You believe in God. The church is supposed to live in you. Some of the world's largest sinners lurk in the church."

After what he said, he got me thinking. I really like never saw Daddy go to church, but he never cheated on Mama. Not that I know of. He just did not treat Mama like she was a queen. On the other hand, Mama was a faithful church goer but had broken one of the Ten Commandments with her promiscuous lifestyle. I really do wonder if God is a myth created by adults to get their children to behave. The feelings I get when I sing praises to God makes me believe he is real. God must be disappointed with me and the life that I'm living right now. I miss my church family though, but I also like my side hustle that I do. I don't think God will be mad at me if I did church choir and sold drugs on the streets. He should understand, right?

CHAPTER 8:

The Devil Gives out Blessings Too

I skipped the normal time I hung out with Nicole and Diamond and went to choir practice early Saturday. I took my brother and sister as well, as Daddy had advised. I felt a bit out of place at choir practice, since it had been a while, and my life had changed so much. Ms. Brenda gave me a nasty look as if I were a threat. I don't know what the hell I did to her. I mean, I'm just a kid. Minster Dean, the choir director, didn't get involved in church drama. He was always focused on the choir and into making us as perfect as we could be. I did wish Mama would come back to church though. The church could heal her, and I felt guilty for my recent lifestyle. We could both use some healing and God's love.

It seems like Christians must be poor and oppressed, and the pastor is the only one with a fancy car. He may have a nice car, but, on the block, I get money and get to live my ghetto dream of buying the cool trendy clothes and the latest shoes. I got money to do and buy whatever I wanted. All I had to do for it was sell rocks, which beat going to church with a bunch of old uneducated folks who prayed to a white Jesus and gave the pastor all their money. After choir rehearsal, we got home to find Mama and Darnell chilling on the living room couch, watching a movie. Mama looked happier with Darnell, and we were kind of happy too. It was as if the whole house was happy. Darnell cooked dinner for us, and we ate together at the kitchen table like one big happy family. Darnell was much nicer; he just didn't have a job which wasn't too bad, as we got to spend more time with him. I wish I could have told him about all the money he could have made on the streets, but I guess he preferred living his unemployed lifestyle.

I got up early the next morning to continue my hustle. To my surprise, the crackheads wake up early too, already ready to get some dope into their system like it was an early breakfast. It's as if they don't even sleep. These crackheads are just waiting and living for their next hit. From the corner of my eye, I could see Henry approaching me.

"Hey, Kind, remember you asked me if there was any more work I could give you? Well, I found a guy that could use us, but he sells heroin," Henry informed me.

"Ok, and..." I said, waiting for more.

"Heroin is a different type of drug, and it sells faster. A heroin is much different from the one's we're dealing with. You have to understand that heroin to heroin user is like their oxygen," Henry said.

He continued, "Heroin addicts are in our business too. They will sell their bodies for money, so they can get their next fix. Heroin addicts will literally kill anyone for their next fix which is why I'm going to need you to be carrying a gun on you. But we got to get the work from my cousin out west in the village...Kind, you got to keep heat on you. How do you feel about this?"

"Well, it definitely sounds scary, but it seems like I can make money fast, right? For a better life?"

"Of course, Kind. You'll be making five times more of what you're making now," he reassured me.

CHAPTER 9:

Summertime in the Chi

Summer in Chicago is always the best even in the projects of Chicago. The rats don't hang in the building in the summer. They're too busy soaking up the beautiful weather outside. People do more barbecues and others sell snow cones. I love buying the coconut snow cones; they're the best. With the money I make, I could start buying Star and Leo some as well. Selling dope really does have its benefits. Now I can treat my brother and sister. I can't remember a time I was ever able to buy something small for Leo and Star. What really makes the summer great is that the days are much longer, and I can get natural Vitamin D from the sun. The summer is always a blast. We pop fireworks every night of the summer, loud music plays from broken down cars in the parking lot. Things are not so bad when living in poverty in the summer. But don't get me started on the winters; it's always so cold, nasty, and depressing, that no one comes outside. Even the dealers move their spots to be indoors. When dealers move their business indoor, it makes things a lot more dangerous and the building starts smelling like straight up drugs—it's disgusting. Winter is also when everyone gets lazy, which makes things in the building ten times disgusting, since no one wants to go outside and take out the trash. They just end up letting the trash pile up in the hallways.

My friends and I don't hangout as much anymore. The SAB crew we made is practically nonexistent. Diamond's been caught up with her new man, Red, who is really controlling. Ever since the two have been together, I've notice Diamond's shape becoming more feminine. They must really be doing something under the sheets. She looks like a grown woman with her flat stomach, small waist, and big booty. Red knows how to keep Diamond away from the crazy-ass dope dealers. I do not think she should be with Red though. But Diamond's mom encourages her to stay with him because that is her means to get money. Red had bought them modern furniture too. Red is a verbal abuser. He is not even that cute either. He has crooked teeth and bad breath. The good thing is that Red is financially stable—I mean, if he stays out of trouble with the law. Honestly, Diamond looks less happy. She was better off selling dope for him and making her own money than sleeping with him and having him give her money.

Nicole and her boyfriend, on the other hand, are like Diamond and Red. He treats her the same way—controlling. She does not sell bags with me anymore either. All she does is sit on the steps and watch him work. He is always trying to let everyone know she is his girl with all the nonsense they do. He takes her shopping but is extremely strict with what clothes he lets her buy. He acts like he's her dad when they really have only a one-year age gap. He is seventeen and she is sixteen. I refuse to let some boys control me. Only God can control me. Henry and Red respect me though because they know I will stand up for myself.

Growing up in the projects, you do not see many happy families. The drug dealers are my American dream; it is the only way I could see myself being able to live nice and get the house and car I have dreamed of. But come to think of it, the drug dealers do not get to live the lifestyle for long because 99 percent of the times, they end up getting locked up or murdered. I'm aware of these consequences, but I got nothing to live for, so I'm enjoying life for as long as I can.

I went back home to get my money. I've been saving to go out west to meet Henry's cousin. Mama and Darnell still look happy together. It's nice to have someone who helps around with the cooking and cleaning in the house. I just can't respect him for not trying to get some bread to feed the family. I got more respect for the drug dealers because at least they're willing to die to support their families. I've got to say that I'm proud of myself because I make more money than Mama and her boyfriend. Mama's been taking temporary jobs every now and then.

I thought about what my daddy had said about women in the projects. He said they were weak, and their families would hand over their daughters for cigarettes, alcohol, crack, and all kinds of things. Daddy said men are natural hunters, and if a household lacks a manly figure to protect the home, then a weak goon will come and take over the house and destroy it. He was good at saying he was the man of the house but could not support his family but wanted Mama to slave away in the kitchen. He's such as hypocrite. He could not even do his part as a man, and he would constantly complain about Mama.

Most of the men in the building seem like they are allergic to making money and immune to taking the welfare check from the women. Diamond was telling me that older men are much better and love to please you. She was telling how good Red is and that he always got her ending up with a major orgasm.

I can always smell Elijah's cool water cologne from a mile away; that's how I know he's close to me.

"Kind, come take a ride with me to the lake?" Elijah asked politely.

I thought for a second. "I can't. I'm about to make a run with Henry."

I thought to myself, *God knows it's the devil tempting me to go for a ride to the lake with Elijah, which would be a good idea.* My mind started to wander to all talks. Diamond was telling me about her sex life. It was getting hot. I thought about the fact that Elijah usually has his music blasting in his car, but he always plays the best slow jams. I snapped back to reality to find Elijah staring at me.

"Yeah. I can't. Sorry, Elijah," I said apologetically.

"Well, page me when you change your mind. I'd like to talk to you about something," Elijah said.

"Alright, I'll catch you later, Elijah," I said, and with that, I walked out. I could feel his eyes on me and his anger at the same time as I walked off.

CHAPTER 10:

Westside

Later, I met up with Henry. I had crackhead Betty to take me out to the village on the westside of Chicago to meet Henry's cousin, Bird. It was my first time on the westside. I knew they are making money selling drugs out here. All I could see was dopeheads lurking around the streets. A baby could sell drugs out here and make money. It was a different world out here. I met Henry, and we were off to make our first purchase. Henry got out of the car and made his way to the black Grand Cherokee Jeep. It was already there when we pulled up. I watched Henry disappear into the back passenger seat of the car for a while. At this point, the paranoia was setting in. I was praying to God this isn't a setup, but thank God it was a success.

The night flew by fast. I gave Henry eight hundred dollars. I couldn't help but continue to feel like I was on another planet. I could see clearly why some people didn't want to leave the projects.

Eventually, a man came out from a car and approached Betty's beat-up Ford Tempo.

Henry introduced me, "This is my cousin, Kind."

He continued speaking to the customer, "My cousin said we are about to make some real money. This shit makes dopeheads zombies. They are not even selling this out south yet."

The man questioned me, "Kind, I heard you are a true hustler. Is that true?"

"I'm already serving in the building, so I know the drill. I will be the first one up to serve," I explained.

"How early, Kind?" he asked.

"Five in the morning. Okay?" I asked with confidence.

He tried to hide his shock, but I could tell he was taken aback and impressed with my answer. Little does he know that I'm hungry and tired of living a poor life.

He continued, "I don't know about that. I'm going to show you how it works. You guys can get more weekly. Also, Kind, you will also have my protection as well. Nobody fucks with Bird. How old are you?"

"Fifteen," I softly said.

"You a cutie, Kind; I'll catch you in two years. Seventeen is the legal age for these perverts I thought." And with that, he was gone.

Henry and I didn't get back from out west till one in the morning. Bird dropped a lot of jewels on me and Henry. I felt empowered, and even if police caught me, being a minor, they wouldn't be able to do much. Bird said, "I got to sell as much as I can before I turn sixteen." When we got back from the westside, I stayed out to try this new product and gave Betty some as well. She let me sell outside her car till six in the morning. Henry was not lying about this heroin. People really are found out all night till morning selling and looking for the stuff to a point that I literally sold out everything.

I heard someone calling my name as I was headed into the building. I turned to find Bird. What the hell was he doing over here so early? *Has he been spying on me*, I thought to myself. My mind began thinking about the pistol I had on me. I discreetly tapped it in my pocket to make sure it was there. Bird was approaching me fast.

"I see you came and got right to work. Just pay attention to your surroundings, always. I know you're a hustler, but people are going to see you as a threat because you're here getting in people's ways. You can't trust anyone in this game—except me. You got it?" Bird said.

"Ok," I said with discomfort.

"You're my ninja, Kind. You remind me of myself. I got into the game at a young age too. Anyways, go get you some rest."

I smiled and tiptoed into my house. Everyone was already asleep. The minute I hit my bed, I was gone. I woke up at around noon to the smell of fried French fries and polish in the air.

CHAPTER 11:

Fatherly Love

I could already tell it was Darnell whipping something up in the kitchen. Darnell was really starting to grow on me. I had developed more of a liking to him because he didn't let Mama sell the food stamps, so we hadn't really run out of food as often as we used to. I watched him from the distance as he danced around the kitchen.

"Come have a seat, Kind." he said.

I perked up in shock that he knew I was there watching him.

He continued, "I know I'm not your father, but I almost was your father."

"What do you mean, Darnell?" I curiously asked.

"Well, your mom and I used to always play together in the sandbox when we were younger. We met again in high school and dated for a while. I'd say a few months, but then we went our separate ways as you can see," he explained.

"Ok, why are you telling me this?" I asked.

"Just listen. During the time, your mom and I were separated, I got Tammy pregnant, but she had a tube pregnancy where the baby was inside the tube. It almost cost her life because we found out too late. In order to save her life, the doctors had to remove her reproductive organs so she couldn't have kids anymore," he explained, biting back tears.

I thought to myself, *Oh so that's why Tammy does not have any kids.* I felt bad. She was always nice to the children in church.

"Anyways, have a seat, Kind."

Darnell made himself and me a plate of hash browns, scrambled eggs, and sausages.

He looked up at me with seriousness and said, "I know what you're doing, Kind."

I tried to hide my anxiety and asked, "Doing what?"

"Look, I'm not judging you. I just want to give you some advice. I just would like you to tell me wherever you are in the building. If you're going to be hustling the streets, just tell me where you are. And please, never try the products," he calmly requested.

I was speechless.

"And please stay close to Elijah. I know he cares about you, and I can trust him to make sure nothing happens to you. But if he tries anything with you, let me know. I've talked to him about that. Alright? You'll let me know if anything happens even though I may not be your dad?" he asked.

"You are the closest thing to a Dad I have ever had, Darnell," I blurted out.

I could not believe what I had just said. I felt my face grow moist. They were tears streaming down my cheeks. I started to realize how much my dad not being around was affecting me. Darnell pulled me in for a warm hug.

When we were done eating, I went to check up on Mama in her room. She was covered in bruises. I was starting to think that Darnell did this to her, but she quickly reassured me and said it was chicken pox.

"Mama, are you going to go to the doctor?"

"Darnell's got things under control. Kind, please don't come into my house past midnight, and don't let anyone know where you are. Have you been hanging out with Elijah?" she asked, her voice hoarse.

"No," I lied.

"Doesn't he like you or something?" she asked between her coughs.

"Mama, he's too old."

"Girl, mentally you are the same age," she said jokingly.

I took a shower and got dressed. After I got done getting dressed, I went to Tikka to get my hair done. It had been so long since her hands have blessed my hair. I wanted her to straighten my hair, but we went for a natural curly hairstyle because she suggested the natural look. As she was doing my hair, she began lecturing me about life and how I don't need to rush to grow up and go off in the street dating a drug dealer. She explained to me why I would not want to live that lifestyle. I was not in the mood to listen to her supposed advice. She went on to explain how she got the scar on her face when she dated one of the top chiefs who was known for messing with a lot of women. Tikka went to Robert Taylor's projects to confront one of the girls, things got messy, and the girl sliced Tikka in the face with a knife. She was eighteen years old at the time. She left the man and found herself stuck with two babies and welfare, but later, Tikka started doing hair and moved to Harvey. She never looked back after that. She does regret having two babies at a young age. I admire Tikka even though I thought she dated a drug dealer because she drove a Range Rover. She's the independent woman I hope to be.

She continued to advise me, "Kind, please keep yourself and save yourself for your husband. I wish I had someone to tell me what I am telling you. Your body is a temple. Don't let these nigga's trick you out of being good. If you ever feel like a man wants to use you, make sure he pays you."

"But isn't that prostitution, Tikka?" I questioned.

"No, making a man pay for using your value is not prostitution. I hate seeing young girls giving it all away for free when these niggas know damn well. So, Kind, if you can't keep your virginity, know what it's worth. These no-good niggas will victimize you but if the correct man loves you, he will wait. Please don't be like your girl Diamond—fucking on a grown man who won't even help her get her teeth fixed. These old niggas stay taking advantage of you young girls because they know you are naïve. Just hold on to your jewels, Kind," she advised.

When Nina was done, I helped clean her shop and paid for her service. I really appreciate the advice Nina gave me. It was something to think about. Mama never gave me this advice. I was thankful her advice came just when I was starting to feel the peer pressure around me to give myself away to the first person who showed interest in me. But Nina was right. I am too young, and I don't want these niggas taking advantage of me. I cannot sin anymore; I've already sinned by selling these drugs. I would be pushing my limit. But how can you not sin when you are surrounded in a building of sinners? Mama has really changed. She knew I was out here selling drugs because I gave her one hundred fifty dollars a week, and she did not care. In one month, I made two thousand six hundred dollars.

It was the fourth of July. I was excited. This was going to be the first time me and my siblings would have the latest fashion on.

CHAPTER 11:

July 4th

Every year we go to my Grandma Ann's house, looking dirty and poor. I got Star's hair braided and Leo a haircut. We all had blue-and-white Jordans on and Tommy fits. Mama took care of herself. We rode the bus to my grandma's house. When we walked in, it was silent. I guess everyone was surprised how nice we looked. My already drunk grandfather broke the silence. He asked Mama if she got a raise on her welfare check. My grandmother ignored him. She told us to come and fix a plate. I was so glad to get out of Grandma Anne's house to go to Granny Rose's house. I stopped at 7-Eleven and served a couple of crackheads on my way there. As soon as I got inside granny's house, she rushed over to the door and cheerfully greeted me. The house was already packed with the whole family celebrating the 4th of July, which I do not agree with celebrating. I believe we should celebrate June 10th. It was the day slaves were given freedom. Why are we celebrating the day whites still had blacks enslaved?

"Kind, you look so pretty. I love your hair. Is that all your hair, baby girl?" she asked as she ran her fingers through my hair.

"Yes, Granny," I said.

"Kind look at you looking all cute and stuff," she praised me.

My granny had three girls and two boys in which my daddy is the oldest amongst them. Tanya is my favorite aunt.

"How you like high school, baby girl?" Granny asked.

"It's okay," I said shyly.

"Come on. Come see your daddy."

My eyes lit up with joy. I knew my daddy would be here. I was so excited to show my daddy my new hairdo and the clothes I was wearing. Granny hollered to my cousin Sky sitting on a comfy sofa in the front living room area.

"Sky, go get Uncle Tony out the basement," she instructed her.

Sky is my cousin who is a year older than me. She's sixteen years old. I was wondering what Daddy was doing in the basement and why she didn't just tell me to go to the basement and get him. I get that I haven't been to her house in a while, but I can go myself. Moments later, my daddy came upstairs from the basement and he seemed off. You would have thought he saw a ghost. He gave me a cold hug and asked about my brother and sister. His hug made me want to burst into tears. Where is Star and Leo?

"They're at grandma's house," I informed him.

"How did you get here?" he asked.

"I walked here, Daddy."

"By yourself?" he questioned.

"Yes, it's fine," I reassured him.

In my heart, I wanted Daddy to come home even though Darnell had been better than him. A woman with at least five kids was following behind; she approached Daddy and me.

"Who is this cutie, Tony?" the light-skinned fat woman asked.

"Nina, this is my oldest daughter, Kind," he answered.

"I thought you told me she was fifteen?" the woman questioned.

I quickly answered, "I am fifteen!"

"Could you please give me one minute, Nina?" Daddy asked her.

Daddy had me and him turn our backs to them, and he softly informed me that those kids were my step siblings. I was shocked. He guided me back toward them.

"Kind, meet your stepbrother and sisters," he said with forced enthusiasm.

Nina continued for him, "This is your sister Karla. She's the same age as your sister Star. And this is Ava, she's fourteen."

Ava has a caramel complexion, and a beautiful body she covered up under modest clothing. She has very strong features and full lips. She has a haircut like Jada Pickett.

"And these two over here are the twins," she continued.

I was so pissed I didn't say anything to them. I left them there and made my way to the kitchen to fix me a plate of food. At that moment when Daddy and that lady were introducing me, I could understand what Tammy was saying, that men leave their family unprotected to take care of another man's kids. I went to the corner of the room with my plate of food and was minding my own business till Sky approached me.

"Kind, are you okay?" Sky asked with concern.

"I'm good," I mumbled.

"You want go to the park?" she asked with hesitation.

"Sure. Let me finish my food first."

"So, your mama's new boyfriend bought you these clothes?" Sky asked trying to make small talk.

"Yeah, he takes really good care of me."

"And your hair. He pays for that?" she asked.

"Yeah," I responded with a mouth full of food.

"I knew your hair was pretty. Your mama just didn't take care of it. But, Kind, please be careful around them men in the buildings. Okay?"

"Yeah, I know," I said without sounding too annoyed.

Ava, Sky, and I arrived at a packed park. Everyone was coupled up. I was dealing with a heartbreak from my father. Cain approached me.

"What's up, Kind? You not speaking? I heard you are working for Elijah now? Is that right?" Cain is my cousin Sky boyfriend. He me a million questions all up in my business.

"I don't work for anybody," I growled at him.

I don't want anyone in my business, and I cannot trust anyone to be telling them what I do. After the stunt my daddy pulled on my Mama, I don't think I could ever trust a man ever again. I'm only focused on the money and surviving these streets.

'Marco, Cain's flunky, approached me.

"Hey, Kind, I love your new style and your natural hair. You look beautiful," he complimented me.

"Thank you. What you been up to?" I asked trying to make conversation.

"Nothing, just chasing the bag. I saw you taking Cain's customers earlier today. I could tell Marco was a wannabe. He lives in Pill Hill. Marco's parents are doctors. How old are you?" he asked.

"Fifteen," I answered without hesitation.

"At least you are honest. Not like these other girls out here who have been lying about their age. Anyways, I'm sixteen," he continued. Marco you right I am not like others girls. To lie about my age. I think this will be my opportunity to have someone work for me. Marco would be perfect since he wants to be down so bad. I feel the vibe Marco is giving me. I know could easily influence him. "Hey, would you like to make more money, Marco? I could use some help. This would be more money for you. You think you can help?" I asked.

"Yeah, if you give me your number," he requested.

One thing I do know about these boys is that their brains is between their legs and egos. Girls mature quicker. Since he's sixteen, he has the maturity level of a nine-year-old. I gave him my number and explained how things work. He looked surprised when I showed him the drugs.

"How did you get all this?" he asked with shock.

"I got connections," I said.

Marco was more of a pretty boy. He has light skin and brown eyes. He goes to Leo Catholic High School. If I were here doing business with Cain, he would beat me out of my money, but Marco, I could control. My dad came and picked up Ava from the park. My anger towards my father for leaving. Just to be with another family. Resurface at the sight of him. How could he leave his family to let another man babysit us? It makes me sick to my stomach. Don't get me wrong; I am happy he left Mamma, and I never want to see them together again, but how could he walk out on his own kids like we are nothing to him and go start off on an already made family? Just as Daddy was about to leave with his stepdaughter Ava, he gave me twenty dollars to share amongst my siblings. I politely declined the money and walked off. I learned that Daddy finally got a job, and all he could give us was twenty dollars. How pathetic.

Later, I met up with Marco at the park and gave him fifty dollars, so he could grab a pager to stay connected. I also gave him three hundred dollars' worth of work. We talked for a bit, but you will not believe what happened between us—we kissed. A French kiss in fact. He was really into it. I just kissed him because I was bored. I know better than to fall for some man. It was time for me to start heading back home. I did not bother getting my cousin Sky. She was somewhere messing around with Cain. Grandma always thought of her mom as a whore because her mom had four different baby daddies. Sky does not even look like her father, Uncle Chris. I tried to stay away from Sky before she starts peer pressuring me into her lifestyle. It was getting dark outside, which was usually the time Daddy would start looking for me to come back home. He did not even offer to take me home. Anyway, I have my Glock 45, and that is all I need.

I arrived at Grandma's house to find Darnell and Mama not there. I soon found out that it was because of a fight between my granddaddy and Darnell. Granddaddy told Darnell to address him as sir, and Granddaddy refused to let Darnell grab a bite out the fridge because he thinks that since Darnell does not want to work, then he must not eat and drink anything at his house either. Darnell let his hotheaded side get the best of him and wacked Granddaddy with a beer bottle. Granddad was rushed to the hospital to get stitched up.

I left Grandma's house and got on the bus to do some side hustling, since nobody cared about my whereabouts. I looked out the bus window to see a happy family lighting fireworks outside. I wished my family were this happy. I reached my stop, and the bus driver showed a bit of concern for me.

"Be careful, baby," he said with a concerned expression. I forced a smile and went my way.

CHAPTER 12:

Down Low

I was going to get this bag and hustle all night, since no one really cared about me. I thought that I better keep myself busy. I headed to Ms. Q's house where everyone was hanging out. Ms. Q was a different type of crackhead. She always kept her house clean. It wasn't littered and disorganized like most of these crackheads' houses. I could tell she was a heroin user because of the dark circles around her eyes and her swollen scabbed up hands. I spotted Nicole on the couch but didn't see Henry, which I though was strange, since they're basically each other's shadows. The house reeked of weed, and I could tell every single person was high off of some combination of drugs. Suddenly, I hear the Holy Spirit speaking to me to be extra vigilant. I saw Elijah hanging in the corner of the room with a group of men.

"You want to hit this joint," some random man said to me with a joint lingering between his fingers.

Elijah saw this and made his way over to me.

"She good, man," Elijah said on my behalf.

"She with you, Elijah?" the man asked.

I could not help but daydream about how good Elijah was looking in his two-piece Coogi suit. My mind quickly snapped back to this man that was offering me a blunt. Why can't these grown men hangout with women their age? Elijah guided me away from the man.

"Have a drink with me," Elijah said.

"Alright," I replied.

"You ready for some Alize Red Passion? This shit going to get you right," Elijah explained.

"Did Nicole have that?" I asked.

"Yeah, and some extra shit too. I mean, look at her," Elijah said.

I looked over to the couch to see Nicole lying there, wasted. I rushed over to check if she is still breathing. Elijah just stood their laughing.

"Don't worry, Kind. Your girl's alive," he said reassuring me.

"You sure?"

"Of course, Kind. I got you. Now, come on," Elijah said.

"Alright," I muttered, unsure.

Elijah dragged me over to a table full of alcohol bottles. I had some of the Red Passion with some snow cone ice. It was really good actually. Elijah and I hung out on the couch for a few till I started to feel his hand on my thigh. I immediately got up and said I got to pee. I ran into a bedroom and hid inside the closet. I heard someone walk into the bedroom and tried to stay as quiet as possible. I peeped through the closet door crack to see Henry and Steve undressing. They were literally having sex right before my eyes. I could not believe it. I wanted to leave this place so badly. Poor Nicole, what am I going to tell her? I thought to myself.

It was a perfect bright and sunny Sunday morning. I took Star and Leo with me to church. Our church has a couple clicks. Those who are really close to the pastor and are a part of the board committee, the wealthy church members who support the church with their money, and then you have us—the poor people who simply attend to worship God. The people at the top of the hierarchy are the ones whose children usually get most of the lead parts in our Christmas programs. Unlike us poor people, for whom it is nearly impossible to become leads. We arrived at the church, and I felt an immediate guilty conscience. I always felt at ease and safe in the house of God. I was greeted with hugs from my choir members. Mr. Dean, the choir director, was excited to see me.

"Kind, there you are girl. Don't you ever stay away this long again. You've got to use the gift God gave you," Mr. Dean said with a smile.

Ms. Beech, one of the mothers on the board of members approached me and expressed how glad she was to see me as well.

"How is your mamma?" Ms. Beech asked.

"She's fine," I replied.

Miss Beech then generously gave my siblings and me a bunch of butterscotch and peppermint candies from her bag. I had Star and Leo sit with Miss Beech while I went to join the choir. I could not wait to sing in the choir. Minister Dean started playing "Just ask in my name"—one of my favorite songs to sing lead. It had been a long time. I sang my heart out. When I was done singing, the whole church was in tears—even Tammy.

After the service, Brenda kept giving me a nasty look. I knew that she knew her daughter's husband left her for my Mama. I just ignored her and did my own thing. I went downstairs with my sibling and had Sunday dinner. It was Ms. Brenda that served us.

"Five dollars," Ms. Brenda said in a cold loud voice.

I gave her a fifty-dollar bill and told her to keep the rest for any family that would like to have dinner. It felt so good to kill her with kindness. I knew she was probably wondering how I was able to afford to give her ten times more money than she asked for. I was hoping any of the kids whose parents only had food stamps would use it instead of going to the corner store to buy chips and juice for dinner. Honestly, it wouldn't hurt the church to give out free food every now and then. Anyways, I am just grateful to be able to put a smile on my brother's and sister's face. They were thrilled to be able to finally have the church's hot cooked meal of fried chicken and baked mac and cheese, collard green, hammock sweet potato, and cornbread. We sat in the small church cafeteria and enjoyed our meal. Ms. Tammy joined us and praised me for my singing.

"How is your mamma doing," Ms. Tammy asked.

"She's fine," I replied.

"Do you see Darnell their often?" she asked.

"Yeah," I said wanting the conversation to end.

Ms. Tammy read my body language and made her way to leave. We stayed for the second service, then walked home after instead of taking the bus. We got snow cones during our walks. My little brother made it fun, since he loves running, so we played with each other on our way back home. My siblings were so excited to walk home. They were just happy to be able to freely be the children that they were. I realized that Mama and Daddy were not going to make my siblings happy, and their happiness was my duty. I can't stop selling drugs. I must provide for them. We walked through the foul-smelling hall of our building and arrived home. Mama didn't even care that we were late and went straight into her room, but Darnell showed some interest.

"How was church?" Darnell asked.

"It was good. The food was delicious too," Star replied with excitement.

"Star, Leo, how about I read you two a bedtime story," Darnell offered.

"Yay," they both said with thrill.

"Kind, you can join us if you want," he said.

"No thanks, Darnell."

I stayed up and talked to God. I asked for his forgiveness because I could not stop selling drugs. I'm sure he understands that it's my only option. I did promise to make sure to pay 10 percent of my tithes.

CHAPTER 13:

Marco's Betrayal

I was so busy with hustling that I did not get the chance to look for Marco. I tried contacting him, but he would not answer my page. I had also been distant with Nicole and Henry ever since I saw you know what, at the party. But you will not believe what I found out. Diamond was pregnant. She was actually happy about it though as if she accomplished something big. It is an accomplishment in my community to not get pregnant before eighteen. But how will Diamond provide for the baby when she's too young to get her own food stamp case for herself.

I found myself hanging out with Leo and Star more. I took on the mother figure since Mama's been losing her mind. Last week, Mamma randomly broke all the dishes in the kitchen. It's as if she was possessed by a demon. Darnell tried calming her down but that did no good. I wish Mama would pull herself together and give me a break by being the strong one, for once. I gave Darnell some money to take Mama out to clear her mind.

I went to the store and ran into Ava, my dad's girlfriend's daughter.

"Ava, what are you doing over here?" I asked.

"What do you mean? I live around here. Building 2432," she responded.

I was shocked. Daddy really moved out our house to live with another family in the projects. *If he lives so close, then why doesn't he come visit us?* I thought to myself. *How disgusting.* Ava gave me a hug and expressed her joy to know we live close to each other so we could maybe hangout in the future. She explained to me how my cousin Sky tried to hook her up with Marco. Ava said she was not having it. Since we are practically sisters. I thought about how Ava could possibly help me get in touch with Marco, so he could pay me the money he owes me.

"Hey, umm...could you page Marco for me please?" I asked.

"Yeah, sure," Ava responded.

He called right back. I could tell Ava was just eager to fit in, so we went to meet Marco together. I told her not to tell anyone. We met Marco at his home in Pill Hill, which is an upper middle class area. My plan was to confront Marco. Ava went to Marco house like I plan. Marco let Ava inside his home. Ava made sure Marco was home alone. She ask him to go the bathroom and let me into the house. Everything went accordingly. Marco thought he saw a ghost or something when I came into his bedroom with Ava.

"You set me up bitch! I am not giving you shit. This little setup you two got going here isn't going to work," Marco said in a raised tone.

This nigga's a dumb motherfucker to think he could take from me. I thought to myself.

"I took a real bitch out with that money," Marco continued.

I pulled out my gun and shot Marco in the head. I could not believe I had just done that. It is as if the devil possessed me in a split second and Ava was a witness to all of it. Ava backed away with her hand raised in surrender.

"Kind, p-p-please, don't shoot me," she pleaded.

"I would never. Come on Ava, let us go."

Ava and I made our way out, abandoning Marco's dead body in the house.

"I wish I had the guts to do that to people who hurt me," Ava said, breaking the awkward silence between us.

"Just stay close to me," I said.

We took the bus and went downtown to Ronnie Steakhouse. We did a little shopping at Carson's too. I realized how much I miss hanging out with my friends, but Ava seems cool.

CHAPTER 14:

Mama

Mama's getting worse. Today she came outside with no clothes on again, so Darnell took her to Saint Bernard Hospital, where they ran tests on her. Darnell and Mama spent the night at the hospital. Darnell came home at around 7:30 in the morning without Mama.

"The hospital is going to keep her," Darnell explained to my siblings and me.

"Why though? Is she okay?" I asked with concern.

"I'm sure she'll be fine. Do not worry. We're all here for each other," Darnell reassured us.

I could not contain my emotions anymore and found myself overwhelmed in the moment that I burst out into tears. I realized that without Darnell, we would not have anyone right now. It would just be me, Star, and Leo. The next day, I left home early to get to work. After I finished hustling, I went to Uncle Chris's baby Mama Candy apartment. To inform her that Mama was in the hospital, Sky my cousin was their when I told her mother the news ,then made my way back home. I got a call from Granny Rose to tell me that she was coming to pick my siblings and me to stay with her because she does not trust Darnell. I told her we were fine, but she refused to listen to me. Later, Sky came over to tell me some important news. We went outside where she told me that Marco was killed in his own home. News that I was aware of.

"They have got Cain in custody," Sky explained.

"Why would they have your boyfriend in custody? Were they close?" I asked, playing dumb.

Cain bullied Marco. Marco started hustling. Cain usually would take his money. Why would you try to hook Ava up with Marco Sky?! Sky looked confused. You are so un loyal Sky, and I walked off. I was angry I killed the wrong person. Marco was too embarrassed to tell me the truth. If Cain gets out of jail, he is a dead man. I cannot go to Marco's funeral, and I killed him. I am not that heartless yet. I went to the hospital to check up on Mamma. She was not looking good at all.

"Hi, baby, is Darnell looking after you guys?" she said with a hoarse voice.

"Yeah, Mama. Granny Rose said she's coming to pick us up to take us with her to her house." I said a bit disappointed.

"Why? Why can't you guys stay with Darnell? Anyways, I am sorry I am in here and cannot take care of you guys. I guess the grudge I have been holding on your father finally took its toll on me. Kind, please promise me you'll never settle for less," Mama said, finishing with a cough.

"I know what you're doing here in the streets. I know you don't have a choice, so I'm thanking your for taking care of the family," she continued.

I was taken aback. This whole time Mama knew what I was doing, and she is telling me only now. Who told her? Did Darnell tell her or something? I was speechless. The whole bus ride home, my mind was trying to decode how Mama new about my side hustle. I got home to find Leo and Star gone. Granny Rose already took them over to her house, I guess, but Darnell was nowhere to be found. I called Granny to let her know that I was on my way over. She told me that she threw Darnell out of the house and took his house keys. I was livid. How could she kick out the only man that genuinely cared for my Mama, siblings, and me? Granny tried to justify her actions by explaining that your immediate family should be the only one living in your mama's house. I called the hospital to tell Mama what Granny had done and discovered that Darnell was with her in her room. He said he would stay with her until she is released. After cooling down, I made my way to Granny Rose's house. Star and Leo rushed over to me and greeted me with a big hug. But the minute I stepped in, Granny Rose started ranting about how Darnell is not our daddy and we should stop acting like it. The couple of days spent at her house were miserable. As an attempt to get out the house, I asked Granny Rose if she could take us to Grandma Anne's, my maternal grandmother, house. She thankfully agreed and dropped us off at her house.

Later, I took a bus ride to go check up on Mama, but I stopped at Harrold's Chicken, and I brought half dark fried extra hard and two grape pop. As I was leaving, I saw Tj, one of the kids from the building, begging for money. I gave Tj five dollars. Tj thanked me so much. I could tell he would have killed for me. That is how bad oppression is in the buildings.

Mama was looking a whole lot better when I got there. The nurse said Mama would get discharged soon, which filled me with joy. Later, I went on the block and split my half with Henry.

"What's wrong little sis? You do not talk to me or Nichole anymore. Did we do something wrong? I heard what happened with your Mama. I am sorry about that. You do not have to go through this alone, Kind," Henry said with concern written all over his eyes.

At that moment, I realized Henry and Nichole love me. I cannot judge her for being a crackhead and him for being a faggot. I love them both. *It's always good to love the ones that love you back,* I thought to myself.

Today's the day Mama's going to get discharged from the hospital. I organized a little welcome back party for her and asked Henry and Nichole to help me set the house up for Mamma. We decorated the house with balloons.

I went to 63rd Halsted and got a marble cake with strawberries and bananas. Henry had crackhead Betty help clean the apartment. Mama's best friend Sheila made potato salad and spaghetti. I stopped over at Grandma's to tell her that Mama would be coming home so she could give me back Leo and Star. But she said she will keep Leo and Star for a couple of weeks so I could help take care of Mama.

The moment had arrived. Mama came in with Darnell and was surprised with all the beautiful balloon decorations and sign that read "Welcome home." Henry, Nichole, Darnell, and Sheila were all the family Mama needed.

"Where are my babies?" Mamas asked.

"Grannies keeping them for a couple weeks to make things easier on you," I explained.

"Why would you do that?" Mama firmly asked.

She acts like I left them with strangers, I thought to myself.

"I want to go get my babies," Mama demanded.

"Okay, Mama. Settle down and eat first," I said, trying to calm her down.

Mama calmed down, and soon we were amidst a house full of laughter and joy. We were just missing Star and Leo. The next week I was going to turn sweet sixteen. I woke up to waffles, bacon with gristle on fried cheese potato with onions, and green peppers, all made by Darnell. I am starting to like Darnell a lot even though he's not my real daddy. He is not even my stepdad. Darnell is the closet thing I have to a father. In the afternoon, we invited Henry, Nicole, Diamond, and Ava to come over. Mama and Darnell made some barbecue ribs and hot links chicken. While they were making the barbecue, I went to go pick up Star and Leo with crackhead Betty. We came home to the wonderful smell of the barbecue. Everyone, including myself, was begging for a plate. So we could get first dibs. Over the meal, Diamond and I talked about her pregnancy journey. Diamond was seven months pregnant now. She told me that her child's father, Red, was locked up which is making things hard for Diamond, since she depended on him for everything financially. *She really should've stayed in the game,* I thought to myself. Reality had started kicking in for her. I bet she regretted being active at such an early age. Me and Diamond had nothing in common anymore. Our lives were completely different. I thought about the fact that Diamond's baby is going to be born into poverty. I mean, who would ever want that for their child? She said she was going to try and finish school, but I doubt that. Henry and Nichole came and joined us. They looked cute in their matching outfits, but I felt bad for Nichole because she does not know her boyfriend Henry is a bisexual person. I cannot bring myself to tell her because Henry is like a brother to me, and I love them both. I am going to mind my own business.

My birthday dinner soon transformed into a party. We had loud music playing by "Hi Five." Some of Darnell's friends came over and started a game of cards. Elijah came as well.

"Hello, Kind? How's everything working with you and Bird?" Elijah asked.

"It's cool. And you?" I asked.

"You know, just sticking strictly to business. I am not trying to be nobody's daddy. He look me up and down."

"I see you didn't get caught up like your girls Nichole and Diamond," Elijah said with a bit of congratulations.

"Anyways, here's your birthday gift from me," he continued. He handed me a small nicely wrapped box.

"Thanks," I said.

Mama was definitely enjoying herself, and I was happy for her. I watched them dance together and couldn't help but smile. Darnell really makes Mama happy. Sky arrived at the party, demanding everyone's attention with her loud hello. *She's such an attention seeker,* I thought to myself. She spotted me on the couch and approached.

"You still mad at me cousin? About Marco?" Sky asked.

I realized that Marco had completely escaped my mind. If I had to kill again, I would do it in a heartbeat. I am not letting anyone get in the way of me being able to provide for my brother and sister. I have gotten so far away from God. It has been a while since I have talked to him.

"Listen, Sky, we cool. Just don't stab me in the back again," I finally responded.

"I just want to say sorry because..." Sky said with sincerity.

Sky went on to talk about Marco's funeral and how beautiful it was. She said she does not talk to Cain anymore and hoped we could hangout more in school. She soon left and gave me a hug. I really appreciated Elijah coming to my birthday party. Before she left, she was teasing me about the fact that she thinks he likes me. Even though he's fine, there is no way in hell I was going to mess around with some grown-ass man.

CHAPTER 15:

Leo Pushed To Death

Suddenly I heard someone screaming...

"Call 911."

"Oh my gosh," another voice said.

I heard more screaming and crying and found that everyone was scrambling out of my apartment to see what was going on outside. I followed close behind and tried to force my way through the crowd of people but could not get through. I just assumed somebody must have gotten shot. Everyone was standing around crying as if they had never seen a dead body before. Elijah was comforting Star, who was hysterically crying.

"Leo is dead," she said, sobbing into Elijah's arms.

"What are you saying, Star?" I said, beginning to freak out.

"He fell out the window after he wouldn't give up his blue freeze pop. He was fighting and got pushed out the window," Star explained.

"What!?" I shouted.

I forced my way through the crowd and peered below the building to find Leo on the ground—unconscious and open eyes. His body twisted like a pretzel. His face was covered with splashes of blood. I collapsed onto the ground and expelled a bloodcurdling scream. I looked over to see Mama doing the same. I pulled myself together, made my way back to the apartment, and got my gun. Growing up in this building killed my moral compass and judgment. I just wanted to shoot something or somebody without delay. Elijah saw me storm out the apartment with the gun and immediately fought for the gun out of my hands. He was able to calm me down, and we waited for the paramedics to arrive. They assumed Leo had a been shot. I corrected the paramedic and told them what Star had told me. Mama could not get a word out to the paramedics due to her endless sobbing. Daddy arrived and made the matter worse. He blamed Mama and threatened to take me and Star away from her.

"You never came to see my brother. Leo hated you!" Star said to Daddy with pure rage.

Daddy went on to blame Darnell for what he thought turned his daughter against him. Darnell quickly shot him back with facts about his action and how Daddy lives minutes away and refuses to visit us and the fact that Daddy never showed concern for Mama when she was in the hospital. Daddy stood there speechless, but his face was full of anger. Then he stormed off.

Darnell was questioning the police, but no one saw anything. There was another boy who died the officer said. The world began to spin around me. I could not believe what I was seeing. Is my brother dead? *No, he can't be,* I thought to myself. He was just here. Earlier that day we were just having fun with each other. I felt my body slowly growing numb. I was overwhelmed to the point that I blacked out.

I woke up the next morning feeling empty. It was not a nightmare. My little brother was dead. Last night was the longest night ever. Star slept with Darnell and Mama. Later that night, we discovered that he was pushed out of the window over a blue fucking freeze pop that TJ wanted. I was not upset with TJ. I blame his parents. TJ's Mama was a dope fiend named Monique that sold her food stamps without giving her son food, which was why he was always hungry. I swear I'm going to kill that bitch next. I mean what kind of mother would let their child scavenge for food out of a garbage. Everyone on the block including Henry was apologizing for my loss. He told he took care of TJ. TJ was the twelve-year-old the officers were talking about. I was numb to it all.

"Thanks Henry...I'm going to whack his mama," I said with a mono-tone voice. We were conversing outside his house. Henry informed me that Diamond went into labor last night and she had twins. Her babies were in the ICU though, hooked up to machines. Henry said he was going to look after her since Red is locked up. It was 9:00 in the morning, and Bird pulled, but we were not due for another drop off today.

"You are all right, Kind? I heard what happened with your brother," Bird asked with concern.

"Yeah," I said halfheartedly.

"How about you hop in the car with me and take a ride with Henry and me?" Bird asked.

I agreed, and we made a stop at McDonalds where Henry got a whole bunch of breakfast meals. Bird gave me two thousand dollars to give Mama toward Leo's funeral. Mama told me that Elijah was already taking care of everything. Mama said she was going to buy a car and get a job so we could get out of this apartment—away from this brutal place. I went back in the car with Bird. He was talking about revenge and something about how Henry moved too soon on TJ.

"Kind, when you are trying to make moves, you can't stay around people who will kill over something like a freeze pop. You do not want to be the girl who got all the money in the hood, or you will be dead before you know it. Surround yourself with people who too busy with their own hustles. Instead of takers," Bird ranted.

"The money we're making should be saved to get our families out of the projects," he advised me and Henry.

"Kind, how much money you got saved? I know you made at least six thousand dollars this summer. How much you got?" Bird asked.

"About two thousand nine hundred dollars. I had my birthday party last night," I answered.

"You had a party for free loaders, and your brother got killed?" Bird stated, making me feel worse.

"Henry, how much you got saved?" Bird asked.

"Five thousand dollars," Henry said.

"That's not bad. But do y'all really want to stay in the projects forever?" Bird asked.

"What's wrong with that? You really don't want to live here anymore?" Henry asked.

"My brother is dead! This place is crawling with fiends and everybody is struggling. It's depressing," I said, trying to keep my cool.

"Now, Kind, if you save like Henry and think like that. You can make selling drugs for what it's worth," Bird explained.

"All I'm saying is that there is a better life out there. You could continue your education and stack your money instead of balling out in material shits," Bird advised.

CHAPTER 15:

Mama Got HIV

We went to a nice restaurant in Boys Town, but it was disgusting at the same time to see men being intimate with each other. I see why the South Side called the North Side weird. I left the table for a moment to go to the restroom, and you will not believe what I just witnessed. I saw my daddy inside another man's mouth. It was just not another man, but it was Uncle Tim. I immediately took a U-turn and went back to the table before he spotted me. I explained to Bird and Henry what I just witnessed, and Bird unexpectedly justified why Daddy was kissing another man. He explained that when you are locked up, it is all you got. I could not bear to hear any more of the awful truth Bird was spitting. *I have to tell Ava,* I thought to myself, and Daddy never been to jail.

Henry walked me to my apartment. We were going to hang out, but all the argument he heard coming from inside, changed his mind. I was dreading to go inside after hearing the voice of Grandma and Grandpa. I braced myself inside to find Grandma and Grandpa coming hard on Mama. Darnell was in the room as well. I went into the living room and told them to get out.

"Kind don't talk to your grandma like that," Mama said.

"Our money comes with our rules," Grandma said, boiling the blood underneath my skin.

"Your money? For what? The funeral? That is already paid for. Grandma, I know you look down on us because we live in the projects, but some people here are like family," I snapped back.

The room fell silent, and with that, Grandma and Granddaddy left. Mama busted out into tears and apologized. I did not think she needed to apologize, but she said she was apologizing for everything that had happened in the past. I told her I knew about Daddy.

"What do you mean?" Mama asked.

"I know what daddy is. Darnell asked Sheila to leave. Sheila knows Mama explained.

Mama went on to reveal that she already knew that Daddy used her as a cover-up for his sexuality. Darnell joined in on the discussion and said,

"From a man's point of view, have you ever seen me argue with your mamma?" Darnell asked.

"No," I answered.

"You know why? Because I don't hate woman. Men should never argue with a woman much less put her down because of her looks. How your daddy treated your Mama comes from an insecure man who is not comfortable with himself. That is why he hid the fact that he's gay," Darnell further explained. Mama voice kept cracking while she was explaining everything to me. I have been sick because your daddy gave me HIV, but I did not know I was infected. I did not find out until I went into the hospital. I will be okay if I take my medication. He had time to divorce me but not time to tell me, he was positive. Kind, please guard your heart and be wise and pray for a spirit of discerning. You have evil people out here who will intentional try to hurt you.

Darnell went on to explain that he and Mama were creeping behind Daddy's back and she ended up getting pregnant with Leo. I was shaking. Leo is Darnell's son.

We got a lot of donations for Leo's funeral. Mama said his funeral colors are blue and white. I realized that I had nothing to wear to his funeral and asked Darnell if we could go downtown to find something. Mama, Darnell, Sheila, Star, and I, all had fun shopping at Carson, but I felt guilty because ideally, I should have missed Leo. After shopping, we went to Ronnie's Steak House. Mama and Darnell have never eaten there before, one of the side effects of being poor. The minute we set foot inside the restaurant, that's when things started to hit us about Leo. We all broke down into tears, and Sheila went home early.

The next day, I woke up at 11 a.m. to find everyone else still sleeping. I cried about Leo and took a bath. Moments later, I knocked on Mama's door, but no one answered so I just left the house to go to the hospital to check up on Diamond and her babies. I overheard one of the nurses talking about how Diamond's visitors have all been eighteen years old or younger and how this is some project lifestyle shit. I went into the room to find Elijah sitting on the couch. We walked to the baby ICU room where Diamond told me she was sorry about Leo as well. We got to the baby ICU and saw her two babies hooked up to the machines. The doctor pulled Diamond to the side. I observed their conversation that resulted in Diamond bursting out into tears. Diamond came to me and told me that the doctor told her that her babies may not make it, but I was taken back by what she added.

"Honestly, I don't want them to." Diamond coldly said.

But then she added, "I love them too much to bring them into a world where they will suffer. I know it sounds fucked up, but it's the right thing."

"It's okay, Diamond. I understand. But you will have the government that will help you take care of them," I said, giving her a hug.

"Doctors said I'm being discharged tomorrow but the babies got to stay."

"Ok, just take care of yourself and watch out for Elijah," I said.

I stopped by Ava's to warn her about my daddy and the fact that he's gay and gave my Mama HIV. She said she wanted to kill him. She said her

Mamma was admitted into Michael Reese hospital and that she will be okay. Her mother took my daddy's keys. We just wanted to go and throw his shit out of the house, so we got Henry and Nicole to help throw Daddy's shit into the dumpster. I spent time on the block with Elijah for a little bit and told him what was going on with Daddy and the HIV ordeal. He suggested I get tested to make sure I do not have it.

"Where would I go?" I asked.

"Board of health. I can take you," he offered.

"Can we go today?" I asked.

"It's too late. We can go first thing in the morning. I swear if he gave that shit to you, I'm going to kill him. You my future, Kind. When the time's right, you are going to be my wife. I know you're young, but I can wait," Elijah said.

"And if my test comes positive?" I added, teasing him.

"I'm still gone make you my wife," Elijah said.

"I'm cool with you waiting but don't fuck with my friends. Diamond is off limits," I threatened him.

He chuckled.

I asked Elijah to take me to the bank so I could open a savings account. I wanted to start saving my money. He explained my Mama would have to do that.

Today's Leo funeral. We all went to Trina's to get our hair done. Mama got a short pixie cut, Star got her hair curled, and I got my hair cut into a bob. We had two white limos. My maternal grandparents did not want to get picked up from the projects. Uncle Chris, Sky, Granny, Auntie, Elijah, Diamond, Henry, Nichole, and Darnell's mama, all came. Ava could not come to the funeral because her mom turned for the worst and was on hospice. Bird brought beautiful flowers. We arrived in the limo to a packed funeral service. Leo was clearly loved. It was an open casket funeral. I was so scared to go up to my brother's casket. When I built the courage, I saw my beautiful brother nicely dressed up in a suit. It was as if he were a sleeping angel. I sobbed at the foot of his casket, full of pain in my heart. Henry and Nicole escorted me back to my seat. I sat in my seat, numb for the remainder of the service as Pastor Turner preached and the choir sang "Safe in his Arms" and "For the good all" by Milton Brunson. Darnell looked terrible. I could tell Mamma was being strong for him. Daddy sat at the back of the seating at the funeral. Everyone knew about what he did living being an undercover faggot and he was scorned for it. I don't think my dad looked up the whole service. The burial was the hardest part. I had so much on my mind. It was so hard to say goodbye. To escape it all, I went to the church bathroom and drank some Mad Dog 2020. Diamond found me and came to comfort me. Her babies had died a day after I went to see her. At this point, we both needed each other.

I went out to the park and drank some more where Bird found me. He asked if I were ok and if I would like to go for a ride. Normally I would say no, but the Mad Dog 22 was really fucking with my head. I agreed, and we went to the lake and sat in his car where I told him I was worried about my AIDS test result. I knew that Bird clearly did not like the fact that Elijah took me.

"Be careful with Elijah. I feel like he is trying to manipulate you. A man doesn't spend his time on nothing he does not want," Bird said.

"I'm still a little girl," I said wit slightly slurred speech.

"I know that, but I don't think he does. I want Kind like you. I love the way you carry yourself. You are a smart girl. You aren't fast like these other girls losing their virginity," Bird confessed.

"And I'm keeping it that way till marriage," I added.

"No, you are not. Just wait till I like on that pussy " the perverted Bird added.

Just like any other girl in this situation, I felt just as uncomfortable.

"Take me home, Bird," I demanded.

Bird dropped me off in front of my building.

"How about a kiss on the cheek? Huh?" Bird continued.

"No!" I said, storming out of his car.

Elijah was waiting outside my building.

"Where are you coming from?" Elijah asked.

"Bird's just dropped me off," I mumbled.

"I don't trust him," Elijah added.

"Why, Elijah? He told me the same thing about you," I said.

"Really? That Nigga do not know me and that is for the better! I'm twenty-four, Kind. That nigga is thirty. A real Chester. He got babies with girls younger than you in the village out west. He is the only dope dealer I know that has been locked up for fucking with a minor, for heaven's sake. Look, I am not trying to control you or tell you what to do, but men are physical, and I know you have been drinking. I just don't want anyone taking advantage of you," Elijah ranted.

"I know Elijah, and I love you for that. I appreciate it," I confessed.

The next morning, I went to go check on Ava. Her mom passed away from HIV. Her brother and sisters are already split up with their dads, since they all have different fathers. Ava's going to stay in their apartment until building manger finds out. Ava opened to me about her uncle raping her when she was ten and that he lives with her grandma. I was speechless and did not know what to tell her or do about it. I already knew she was in so much pain from losing her mom. She is the only one whose dad is in prison. He does not get out until two more years. Her dad had a lot of pull in the streets. I spent time with Ava for a bit, then later, went back home and told Mama what had happened with Ava. She said Ava could stay with us. Mama told me that a lawyer came by with a lawsuit because Chicago Housing Authority should have had the vacant apartment locked up. They are going to want to settle, which I had hoped for. It would be our only way out of the projects, then we could move to Hazel Crest or something.

CHAPTER 16:

Wages of Sin Is Death!

Today's my first day of sophomore year. I got blonde highlights in my hair and got it pressed into a bob. Darnell helped me pick my classes which consisted of African American studies, chemistry, and track. Diamond transferred to Phillips, and Nichole dropped out of school; drugs got the best of her. Ava and Sky also went to Phillips High School, although Ava wanted to come with me but could not, since Mama is not her legal guardian. I just did not like the fact that I was going to enter sophomore year with none of my crew and with a lot of Robert Taylor's home project kids. Anyways, I enjoyed my first day in my African American class. It is going to be an interesting school year. The teacher of that class, Mr. Hay, said that he teaches this class because he wants to change the minds of young Black kids who grow up in poverty and educate them about life beyond welfare. He taught us a lesson about life after slavery, where Blacks did not have welfare and had to work. Blacks had built their own communities. He told us that there was even a black wall street in the early 20th century. With the little information, we learned. I was already excited for the class. I could tell everyone had already created their friend groups. I ate lunch alone, which I did not mind. The lunchroom was loud, so I went to the library to eat my lunch instead and started on my homework. Mr. Hay said that a lot of our assignments would require research because the school books had been whitewashed.

After school, Darnell picked me up. Mama should be getting the insurance check soon, so we can start looking for a house. I want us to move to the suburbs, but Mama believes the suburbs are racist and that we do not know anyone there. She feels safer here. *But how are we safe when my little brother was thrown out the window,* I thought to myself.

Later in the day, Ava and I spent time together for a bit and did some catching up. She said she liked her school and that she was going to try out for the swimming team.

"I don't think I'm going to be able to hustle anymore. I might just have to go live with my grandma and fight my uncle off because she gets a check for me now," Ava explained.

"Please don't say that, Ava. That would devastate Mama and knowing what your uncle is capable of. Don't worry, we are about to get that settlement," I reassured her and gave her a long hug.

She said she has lunch with Diamond and Sky. Poor Star did not even go to school her first day. She had a difficult morning. Darnell and Mama do not want us to move out of the neighborhood, so she is looking to buy a building in the neighborhood. We must move because CHA will not let us stay because of settlement. We think we found a nice two flat building on 45th King Drive where we could try and be one happy family again with a new addition—Ava.

The past few weeks of school have been great. I learned so much about the African American culture and joined the track team. I discovered that I'm a fast runner and earned a nickname from the coach. Speedy K. When I was on the track field, I used it as an opportunity to run away from my reality. I was running as therapy for Leo and Daddy.

Today's Friday, and we have officially found a building to move into after they finally released the check. My daddy tried petitioning the court to receive half of the settlement, but Daddy never signed Leo's birth certificate.

He never signed a birth certificate. Out of fear of child support. We all have my mamma's last name. He has not once tried to contact his daughters. The judge knew better and denied his request. She said Mama and Daddy got an official divorce. Mamma is not required to give daddy nothing. She got five hundred thousand dollars from the settlement and gave Darnell one hundred thousand. She also gave Grandma fifty thousand. She bought herself and Darnell a Benz too.

On our last days in the apartment, Star, Ava, and I all slept in a small twin-sized bed. No one wanted to sleep in Leo's room, so we started to share a room. Star tossed and talked in her sleep. She kept having bad dreams about Leo and would always say "Leave Leo alone" when she was sleeping. We would always have to wake her up out of it, she still would cry.

The next day, Star refused to go to school because she felt scared, but Mama asked Darnell to take her. Meanwhile Elijah waited outside for me in his black 1996 Monte Carlo to take me to school.

"Did you eat breakfast?" Elijah asked.

"Yeah. Darnell cooked," I answered.

"How are things going back at school?" He asked.

"It was good. I'm going to have to stop selling drugs. I don't have the time, and I don't care about it anymore. It is not my lifestyle. I can do better," I explained.

"Alright. I understand. Kind, I want better for us. I mean it. You are my girl," he sweetly told me.

Elijah gives me hope for love and marriage. I want a husband that I could be myself with and feel comfortable sharing anything, and I expect he would do the same. I could see Elijah and me building toward that.

It was a moving day. Elijah, Henry, and Darnell helped us load boxes into the moving truck. I felt sad to leave because there are memories of Leo that lie within these walls. My reminiscing was interrupted by a loud bang followed by countless more. I ran through the hallway to find Darnell, Elijah, and Henry lying on the hallway stairs in a pool of blood. It looked like gun-shot wounds. I screamed for someone to call 911 and immediately went to their sides to try and stop the bleeding.